HELLO! WELCOME TO THE FABUMOUSE WORLD OF THE THEA SISTERS!

Thea Sisters

Hi, I'm Thea Stilton, Geronimo Stilton's sister! I am a special reporter for _The Rodent's Gazette_, the most famous newspaper on Mouse Island. I love traveling and meeting new mice all over the world, like the Thea Sisters. These five friends have helped me out with my adventures. Let me introduce you to these fabumouse young mice!

Colette has a real passion for fashion. She loves to design her own clothes in her favorite color, pink.

Violet loves studying and learning new things. She is a fan of classical music and dreams of becoming a famous violinist someday.

Pamela loves pizza so much she eats it for breakfast. She is a skilled mechanic who can fix just about any motor she gets her paws on.

PAULINA is shy and loves to read about faraway places. But she loves traveling to those places even more.

Nicky is from the Australian Outback, where she developed a love of nature and the environment. This outdoors-loving mouse is always on the move.

Thea Sisters

Thea Stilton

MOUSEFORD ACADEMY
LIGHTS, CAMERA, ACTION!

Scholastic Inc.

Copyright © 2011 by Edizioni Piemme S.p.A., Palazzo Mondadori, Via Mondadori 1, 20090 Segrate, Italy. International Rights © Atlantyca S.p.A. English translation © 2016 by Atlantyca S.p.A.

The publisher does not have any control over and does not assume any responsibility for author or third-party websites or their content.

GERONIMO STILTON and THEA STILTON names, characters, and related indicia are copyright, trademark, and exclusive license of Atlantyca S.p.A. All rights reserved. The moral right of the author has been asserted. Based on an original idea by Elisabetta Dami.

www.geronimostilton.com

Published by Scholastic Inc., 557 Broadway, New York, NY 10012. SCHOLASTIC and associated logos are trademarks and/or registered trademarks of Scholastic Inc.

Stilton is the name of a famous English cheese. It is a registered trademark of the Stilton Cheese Makers' Association. For more information, go to www.stiltoncheese.com.

No part of this publication may be reproduced, stored in a retrieval system, or transmitted in any form or by any means, electronic, mechanical, photocopying, recording, or otherwise, without written permission of the copyright holder. For information regarding permission, please contact: Atlantyca S.p.A., Via Leopardi 8, 20123 Milan, Italy; e-mail foreignrights@atlantyca.it, www.atlantyca.com.

ISBN 978-1-338-05282-4

Text by Thea Stilton
Original title *Ciak si gira a Topford!*
Cover by Giuseppe Facciotto
Illustrations by Barbara Pellizzari (pencils) and Francesco Castelli (color)
Graphics by Chiara Cebraro

Special thanks to Beth Dunfey
Translated by Anna Pizzelli
Interior design by Kay Petronio

10 9 8 7 6 5 4 3 2 1   16 17 18 19 20

Printed in the U.S.A.   40
First printing 2016

LET'S MOVE THOSE TAILS!

The sun was just rising over Whale Island, warming the chilly night air. A light FOG still hung above the houses like a cloud of freshly grated mozzarella.

While the rodents on the rest of the island were slowly stretching their tails and rolling out of bed, the students up at Mouseford Academy were already hopping with activity.

Colette, Nicky, Pam, Paulina, and Violet — five mouselets known as the Thea Sisters — were just about done getting dressed. They were in Colette and Pam's room, which was messier than a muskrat den. Leggings and T-shirts and shoes were scattered everywhere.

While Colette was **FIXING** Paulina's fur-do, Violet and Pamela were picking out what they'd wear that night. Nicky was trying to shut her overstuffed suitcase.

"Perfect!" said Colette as she poked one last barrette into Paulina's fur.

"Tonight is going to be absolutely **fabumouse**," Nicky exclaimed. She pushed one paw down on her **SUITCASE**, finally managing to close it.

Hmm . . .

All done!

"You said it!" Pam replied happily.

There was no doubt about it — the Thea Sisters were about to have a **once-in-a-lifetime** adventure. That night, they would be traveling to Los Angeles to attend the **WORLD** premiere of *Two Mice in the Moonlight*, the latest blockbuster film starring the famouse actor Dylan Delaratt!

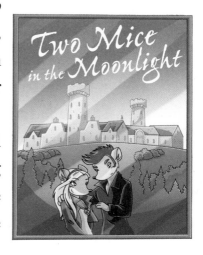

"Are you ready?" asked Connie. She was standing in the doorway with the other members of the Ruby Crew.

"Yep, that's everything," Colette replied, zipping her **PINK** suitcase. "Let's make like a cheese wheel and roll!"

"Is that **all** the luggage you're bringing?"

Paulina wondered. "Just the one suitcase?" She couldn't stop a look of SHOCK from crossing her snout.

You see, Colette was famouse for her passion for fashion. She didn't even like to go to class without a change of clothing!

"Oh, no, don't be ridicumouse! That's just my fur spray and snout cream. There's the rest of my luggage," Colette replied, pointing to a **HUGE** trunk at the foot of her bed.

Nicky, Pam, Paulina, and Violet burst out **LAUGHING**. Now *that* was the real Colette!

As they left campus, Colette, Nicky, Pam, Violet, and Paulina exchanged **LOOKS** of excitement. All five friends were thinking back to the day this ADVENTURE had begun. If you want the full tale, keep reading!

A FEW MONTHS EARLIER ... o o o

Classes had ended for the day, and the Thea Sisters were relaxing in Nicky and Paulina's room.

Violet was practicing her violin, filling the room with a SWEET MELODY.

Colette was reading a book, Nicky was StretCHiNG her paws on the floor, and Paulina was setting up her laptop.

"Anyone up for a quick SCAMPER into town?" Pam asked, glancing out the window. "It's so nice outside."

Nicky grinned. She knew Pam well. And she understood that when her friend suggested a quick scamper into town, she had something special in mind.

"Pam, do you need to order a spare

part for your jeep?" Nicky asked.

"Well, to be honest . . . yes," Pam admitted. "And afterward, I thought we might stop for a slice of pizza. I'm starving!"

Violet laughed. "I'll go with you. I've practiced enough today," she said, putting her VIOLIN away. "And now it's my turn to be honest . . . I'm hungrier than a tomcat at feeding time!"

So Violet and Pam headed away from campus. But getting to the town square was no day at the cheese shop. All the streets in town were jammed with traffic. The harbor was crowded with boats, and the STREETS were crammed with rodents.

At last, the two mouselets reached the Thrifty Rat, their favorite store. By now, Violet and Pam knew something was up. They had never seen the place so packed.

The store's owner, Tamara, was behind the counter, running back and forth like a gerbil on a treadmill.

"What's GOING ON?" Pam asked. "What's with all the rodents everywhere?"

"You mean you don't know?" Tamara replied, giving a bag to a customer.

"Today the . . . yikes, the glasses . . . are coming to Whale Island!"

"What do you mean, the glasses are coming?" Violet asked, baffled.

CRASH! CRASH! CRASH! CRASH! CRASH! CRASH! CRASH!

The sound of broken glass interrupted her. As Tamara's assistant, Cammie, was helping a customer, she had brushed against a floor **LAMP**, which bumped into a spare tire, which knocked into a statue, which tipped onto some glasses, shattering them to *pieces*.

"When the store gets busy, Cammie gets even **CLUMSIER** than usual," said Tamara, shaking her

snout. "And the mayhem is only going to increase once they start **filming**!"

"Filming?" Pam asked, curious. "Now I'm more lost than a lab rat in a maze! Just who exactly is coming to Whale Island?"

"Why, a movie crew!" Tamara replied. "Didn't I say that?"

"That's right!" Cammie put in. "They're filming *Two Mice in the Moonlight*, the latest movie with Dylan Delaratt and Kiki Cattail!"

"Some of the SCENES will be filmed right here on — watch the CANDLES,

Cammie! — Whale Island," Tamara went on, shaking her snout.

"Oops . . ." muttered Cammie, hastily picking up the CANDLES she'd knocked onto the floor.

Tamara sighed. Then she turned to Pamela and Violet. "Did you come to buy something?"

"Um, yes, but no worries, we'll come back when things calm down," Pamela said.

Pam's jeep could wait. But the two mouselets couldn't wait to give their friends the scoop!

A ROMANTIC STORY

Back at **MOUSEFORD**, Violet and Pam scurried to find their friends. They couldn't wait to share the BIG NEWS with the other Thea Sisters.

"Wow!" Paulina exclaimed when she heard. "I wonder what kind of movie it is."

"I'll bet it's an adventure film. Whale Island is the perfect setting!" Nicky chimed in.

"Or maybe it's a musical," Violet said.

Colette giggled. "Oh no, you mouselets have got it all wrong! It's going to be a love story. *Two Mice in the Moonlight* is the third **NOVEL** in Melanie Mousington's bestselling trilogy. It's the story of Victor and Summer, two young sweethearts," she explained. "One of the most romantic scenes takes place in an old **castle**. That's where Victor first declares his feelings for Summer!"

"How do you know so much about this?" Violet asked, surprised.

Colette grinned like the cat who swallowed the canary. "Because last week I was sick

Interesting!

with the FLU, and I caught up on all my favorite magazines! It's been all over the headlines."

The mouselets started **speculating** about the arrival of the movie's two stars, Dylan Delaratt and Kiki Cattail. The young stars were enormousely popular.

"I wonder what they're like in the fur," Nicky said dreamily.

"The magazines I read say Dylan is really moody, and Kiki is a bit of a **snob**," Colette reported knowingly.

"They're the same age as us, but since they're movie stars, they live such glamorous lives!"

Nicky pointed out. "We probably won't even see them once they get to the island. I'm sure they'll have bodyguards and limos and stuff."

"I'll bet you're right, Nick," Pam agreed. "But I still **HOPE** we can get a closer look at how a **MOVIE CREW** works."

"Maybe we'll even get to see part of the shoot," Paulina added.

Just then, Tanja **poked** her snout into the room. "Mouselets, let's head down to the Great Hall. The headmaster is about to make an announcement!"

A SPECIAL ANNOUNCEMENT

Once the Great Hall was filled with mouselets and ratlets, Headmaster Octavius de Mousus began to squeak.

"This is an IMPORTANT day," he said. "Some of you may already know that a MOVIE CREW has just arrived on Whale Island. They will be shooting the film *Two Mice in the Moonlight* right here at Mouseford Academy —"

The mouselets and ratlets all burst into a round of applause.

CLAP, CLAP, CLAP!

You see, MANY of the students were fans of Melanie Mousington's **trilogy**. The thought of their favorite book

series coming to life at their school was a total *thrill*.

"Excuse me, but I'm not finished," the headmaster said sternly, trying to bring his students back to **ORDER**. "As a matter of fact, Ms. Mousington set a key scene here in our **school**. She drew inspiration for her novel from the beloved halls of Mouseford Academy."

There was another **round of applause**, this time louder than before.

"I didn't know that!" Colette whispered to the other Thea Sisters.

I didn't know that!

"Maybe that part was in one of the magazines you don't read," Nicky replied with a **wink**.

The headmaster waited for all the WHiSPeRS to die down.

Then he began **squeaking** again. "I *still* haven't finished! I've called you here to tell you that you will all have the opportunity to attend the filming!"

At that, all the students were squeakless. They were shocked into silence.

The headmaster grinned. "Now you can **clap**!"

The students' last round of applause was the **loudest** one yet.

As the students filed out of the Great Hall, the Thea Sisters and their FRIENDS stopped in the hallway to chat.

"I can't believe Mouseford is going to be the setting for a movie!" Tanja exclaimed.

I'll get to check out all the costumes!

"I know! It's **amazing**!" Colette agreed breathlessly. "I can't wait to talk to a real costume designer. I have *soooo* many questions. Like, how do they choose the FABRIC and COLORS for the costumes? And how do they create each movie's unique style? And how do they —"

"*SLOW DOWN*, Colette," Violet said, laughing. "You're talking faster than my uncle Quentin P. Quicksqueak! Make sure you don't frighten off the costume designer, okay?"

Each of the Thea Sisters was excited about a different PART of the movie shoot. Violet wanted to learn how the SOUND TECHNICIANS did their work, Paulina wanted to learn how to make special effects using CGI, and Pam was dying to watch the SET CONSTRUCTION.

But most students at Mouseford were more interested in meeting the two famouse ACTORS than learning how movies were made.

"Can you believe it?" Alicia squealed. "We're going to meet Dylan Delaratt in the fur!" She was more **excited** than a mouseling on Christmas morning.

"He's so DREAMY," Zoe said with a sigh.

"I know," Tanja said in agreement. "I just adored him in *Mouse Overboard*."

I love Melanie Mousington's books!

"I really hope we can get his autograph," Elly put in. "Maybe he'll even squeak to us!"

Ruby tossed her fur. "Are you kidding me? Dylan Delaratt is a **HUGE** movie star. There's no way he'll waste his time talking to an ORDINARY FAN like you . . ."

Elly's snout fell. Her SAD expression made Pam chew her whiskers. "Don't listen

to her, Elly. I'm sure Dylan Delaratt will be HAPPY to meet a fan like you!"

Pam steered Elly away from the Ruby Crew and brought her over to the Thea Sisters.

Are you kidding me?

Elly **smiled** at Pam, and the mouselets began chattering as cheerfully as chipmunks. The day was way too **special** to let Ruby ruin it!

WELCOME TO THE ACADEMY!

Over the next few days, there was nonstop excitement on the Mouseford campus. The *Two Mice in the Moonlight* crew had arrived, and the Thea Sisters didn't want to miss a chance to check out the **set**. The movie world was **COMPLEX**, and there was lots and lots to learn!

After days and days of setup, it was finally time for the shoot to begin. The only ones missing were . . .

"The actors! They're landing!"

Pamela exclaimed. She scurried to the heliport with her friends.

The entire Mouseford Academy staff was

there to meet the actors and the director. Students crowded around as well, eager to greet the *famouse* guests.

As the helicopter touched the ground, the rodents' eager WHiSPeRS died down. An expectant hush fell over the crowd. But as soon as the cabin door opened to reveal a smiling Kiki Cattail, the silence was broken and there was a roar of applause.

"Welcome to MOUSEFORD," the headmaster said, shaking PAWS with the young actor.

I'm so excited!

Kiki smiled at the warm welcome. She greeted the academy's professors, and then approached the students. "FINALLY! I've really been looking forward to coming to Mouseford," she said, looking around CHEERFULLY.

The students were surprised by Kiki's behavior. Everyone had been expecting a **COLD** and **STANDOFFISH** star.

It's so nice to be here!

Instead, Kiki seemed warm and friendly. She was obviously an outgoing mouselet.

While Kiki was chatting with the students, the director, Charlie Cinerat, scrambled off the helicopter and ran to hug Professor Plotfur, the academy's drama professor.

The two ratlets had worked together in the past, and they'd become GOOD friends.

While everyone was **busy** with introductions and small talk, the last passenger strolled off the helicopter. It was Dylan Delaratt.

The young actor greeted the crowd with a **SHY** smile. He looked a little embarrassed by the *heartfelt* welcome from his fans. When he noticed the ratlet's SHYNESS,

Oh...hi.

the headmaster approached the star with a SMILE.

Nicky was watching the scene from the sidelines. "It doesn't look like Dylan is very **HAPPY** to be here," she whispered to her friends.

"And I'll bet he'll be even less happy once the headmaster starts telling him the history of Mouseford Academy in detail, starting with its founding **six hundred years ago**!" Pam joked.

Ha, ha, ha!

A FUN AFTERNOON

Once the two young actors had arrived, the atmosphere around the academy turned FESTIVE. A group of friendly, curious students surrounded the two stars. Everyone wanted to get to know them.

Kiki turned out to be a lovely mouselet, ready to chat and laugh with anyone. But unfortunately, you couldn't squeak the same of Dylan. He didn't seem interested in making friends with anyone.

"Would you like a TOUR of the campus?" Paulina asked Kiki and Dylan.

"Oh, yes, what a great idea!" Colette exclaimed. "The sun is about to set, and the light in the academy's gardens is really beautiful at this hour."

Before Dylan and Kiki could reply, Ruby cut in. "Why would Kiki and Dylan want to go on a **boring** old walk around campus? I'll bet they'd rather rest before tonight's party!"

"What PARTY?" Kiki asked, frowning.

"Oh, just the party I'm hosting in your

The academy looks fabumouse at sunset!

HONOR on my family's yacht," Ruby explained, looking smug. "It's swankier than soft cheese! You're welcome to stay there during the shoot. I know movie stars like you are used to *elegant* and ex.clusive places, and I'm sure you won't be comfortable in the academy's shabby old dorm rooms."

The Thea Sisters exchanged **glances**. As usual, Ruby was quick to show off!

"Oh, thank you, Ruby, but we've had enough of parties and *luxury* hotels," answered Kiki, shooting Dylan a swift look. "We'd rather take a walk and stay here on

CAMPUS. You see, it's nice for us to be with ratlets and mouselets our own age. We want to take **ADVANTAGE** of the opportunity to hang out with other mice like us."

Kiki's words surprised everyone, including Ruby. "Oh, sure, it's no fur off my snout," she

We've had enough of fancy places!

sniffed, trying to act CASUAL. "Whatever you want."

Whatever you want . . .

Kiki looked at Paulina and smiled. "So, how about that tour of the campus?"

The **RATLETS** and mouselets headed toward the garden. Ruby decided to tag along with the group. It wasn't every day that such important guests came to visit Mouseford, and she wasn't about to let the Thea Sisters hoard them like a fresh pack of cheese curls!

AROUND MOUSEFORD

Like their classmates, the Thea Sisters were **PROUD** to study at Mouseford Academy. The **HISTORIC** institution was like a second home to them. As they led Kiki and Dylan along the **HALLWAYS**, they realized that each room held special **memories**. Sometimes these memories were ancient legends from the academy's past, but there were also many tales in which the mouselets were the **main characters**.

"This is where we solved the mystery of the dragon's code," said Pam. "It's a great story! We'll tell you about it sometime, if you're not too busy."

"And this is a great spot for jogging," said

Nicky, pointing to the path around the garden. "I run here every day."

"I love *running*," Kiki said. "But my favorite sport ever is **SURFING**."

Wahoo!

Nicky's eyes **LIT UP**. "Really? I love surfing, too!"

Not far from them, Colette and Paulina were **CHATTING**. "I'm so happy Dylan and Kiki decided to stay at the academy instead of sleeping on Ruby's **YACHT**. Now we'll have some time to get to know them," Paulina said.

"Kiki is SWEETER than cheese dumplings with syrup on top," Colette said.

"But what about Dylan?" Paulina said.

How strange . . .

"He seems like a *snootysnout*. Check it out: He's walking next to Connie without saying a word to her!"

Colette **watched** Dylan for a minute. The ratlet was scurrying alongside Connie in total *silence*, his **paws** in his pockets.

"You know, Paulina, I don't think he's snooty," Colette said earnestly. "My **rodent's intuition** is telling me there's something else going on."

During the stroll around the grounds, Dylan ended up next to Connie the entire time. He realized right away that she wasn't like one of his usual **fans**, and that made him relax around her. She hardly glanced over at him — she just scampered

along quietly like being next to a big movie star was no big deal. She didn't seem **excited** about it at all.

The truth was, Connie only liked **HORROR** flicks. She barely knew who Dylan Delaratt was. But when she met him, she thought he seemed **INTERESTING** and a little mysterious, too. Connie decided she wouldn't mind being **friends** with him. But whenever she tried **TALKING** to him, he only grunted. After a minute or two, Connie **GAVE UP**.

Dylan gathered enough courage to squeak at the end of the walk, as **TWILIGHT** began to fall.

"In the **MOVIE** that I just finished making . . ." he began.

But before he could finish, Connie **CUT HIM OFF**. "Sorry, but I don't think I've seen any of your movies," she said. Then she walked away, **ANNOYED**. It had taken him forever to squeak up, and when he finally had, all he wanted to talk about was **HIMSELF**!

In the movie I just made . . .

Sorry, I haven't seen any of your movies.

Connie was sure Ruby was right about Dylan. He probably saw her as one of his many fans, CRAZY about him and all his movies, and she didn't want to waste her time on someone as self-absorbed as that.

As he watched Connie walk away, Dylan realized she'd misread his intentions. He'd just been trying to think of something to say to her. "She probably thinks I'm just a big SHOW-OFF who doesn't know his Muenster from his mozzarella!" he mumbled to himself, sighing.

THE ADVENTURE BEGINS

The next morning, the Thea Sisters **met** up with Kiki and Dylan. The headmaster had asked them to escort the two stars to the set.

Colette, Nicky, Pam, Paulina, and Violet wanted to watch the rehearsal before the filming began. Each mouselet had figured out the best way to prepare for the big day. Colette had relaxed by doing her fur, Nicky had gone for a short run, Pam had a **healthy** breakfast, and Paulina had relaxed by taking a long walk.

So relaxing!

The only one who was STILL in bed was . . .

"Violet!" Nicky exclaimed. "Wake up, sleepysnout!" She strode into her friend's **room** and yanked off the **COVERS**.

"I'm up!" Violet cried, **STUMBLING** out of bed. "Let's go!"

Nicky surveyed her friend from snout to tail. Violet looked like something the cat had dragged in. She was still in her pajamas, she was **RUBBING** her puffy eyes, and her fur was sticking **UP**.

"Are you sure you're **READY**?" Nicky asked with a laugh.

"**YES!** I'm ready!" Violet said. Then she glanced in the mirror. "Uh, I should probably get **DRESSED** first . . ."

The other Thea Sisters were waiting with Kiki and Dylan outside Colette and Pam's room.

"Today you can watch the stuntmouse practice," Kiki told Nicky and Violet as they joined the group.

Come with us. We'll take you to the set.

"**Cool**," Nicky exclaimed. "It'll be **amazing** to watch him at work."

The mouselets looked at one another, surprised. Nicky was very well **INFORMED**, but the other Thea Sisters had no idea what a stuntmouse did.

"The **STUNTMOUSE** is an

42

ATHLETE who stands in for the star during complicated and sometimes dangerous scenes," Dylan explained.

Nicky nodded. It was nice to see Dylan was FINALLY getting more comfortable around them.

"Let's move those paws!" Pam exclaimed. "I don't want to miss the shoot!"

At that moment, the door to Ruby's room swung open, and the Ruby Crew walked out. But Ruby, Connie, Alicia, and Zoe didn't seem interested in Dylan, Kiki, and the Thea Sisters. They scurried by without even waving a paw.

"I'm sorry, I don't want to go to the set anymore," Dylan said suddenly.

"What do you mean, you don't want to go anymore?" Kiki asked. "Did something happen? Why did you change your mind?"

The Thea Sisters were more confused than a pack of cats in a dog kennel.

Until a few moments ago, Dylan had seemed cheerful, yet now he suddenly looked grouchier than a groundhog.

"I just remembered that I have an APPOINTMENT," the ratlet explained.

"What's up with him?" asked Pam, watching Dylan scamper away.

Kiki shrugged. "He'll catch up with us later." Then, with her usual smile, she said, "COME ON, LET'S SHAKE A TAIL."

A BiG FAMiLY

In the days before Kiki and Dylan's arrival, the stage crew had worked nonstop to make sure everything would be ready in time for the film shoot.

Although the Thea Sisters had OBSERVED the crew preparing the set day after day, they were still surprised when they saw how their campus had been transformed. It was as if they had stepped into another place and time!

More to the right...

Down by the North Tower, there was a lot of activity.

Charlie Cinerat and the director of photography

were walking around the garden, choosing the *best angles* to shoot from. The set designer was putting the finishing touches on the sets, and the costume designers and **makeup artists** were making sure the actors were ready to roll.

While the Thea Sisters looked around in *wonder*, Kiki said hi to all the rodents working on the set.

"You have a lot of **friends** here," Colette said.

"That's right," Kiki replied, heading for a nearby **BENCH**. "I'm just crazy about all the rodents who work with us. We spend so much time together, we're like a big family."

That big family accepted Kiki's new friends with open paws.

The Thea Sisters soon found themselves swept up in the activities that interested

them most. Colette met Jeanette, the costume designer. It took her a moment to feel comfortable, but once she'd gathered up her **COURAGE**, she told Jeanette what she thought of the costumes for the scene. Soon the two rodents discovered they agreed about the adjustments that needed to

The color of the dress really suits her!

Yes, I completely agree.

be made, and they were chatting away like old pals.

Meanwhile, in practically **NO TIME**, Pam had won the trust of Phil, the head cinematographer.

Paulina was observing the **SPECIAL EFFECTS** team, and she'd already learned what you really needed to create a breathtaking movie: a **computer** and a lot of **imagination**.

As for Violet, she'd met a kind rodent named Peter and discovered a job she hadn't known about: the **Foley artist**. Peter was in charge of adding and removing sounds from the finished film.

As she waited for the stuntmouse rehearsal to begin,

Cool sound effects!

Nicky stayed by Kiki's side. She was helping her new friend run lines.

"**YOU'RE SO GOOD**," Nicky said. Kiki's line reading was so beautiful, it made Nicky's eyes fill with tears. "I'd love to have **TALENT** like yours!"

"Talent is important, but you really need commitment if you want to learn to do something well," Kiki replied. "I love acting, but sometimes it can be harder than finding a cheese slice in a haystack!"

Nicky laughed. Kiki was talented and modest, and she also had a good sense of humor!

A QUICK-THINKING RESPONSE

Before the rehearsal began, the Thea Sisters gathered **AROUND** Kiki so she could tell them the story of Melanie Mousington's *novel*. That way, they'd be able to understand what was going on in the scene they were about to see.

"Two Mice in the Moonlight is the last installment in a trilogy. The books tell the *love* story between Victor and Summer, two young rodents who grew up in a small town in the country," Kiki began. "At first, they seem very different from each other: Summer has a sunny personality, while Victor is very quiet

and MYSTERIOUS. The scene the stuntmouse is rehearsing is a key moment in the story. Victor **LEAPS** from a tower to save Summer. When he leaps, she realizes he has **MAGIC** powers."

As Kiki told the story of Victor and Summer, her eyes shone with affection for the characters. The Thea Sisters listened in SILENCE, completely absorbed.

"It's so romantic!" Colette sighed, wiping away a **TEAR**.

What a romantic story!

Just then Charlie Cinerat's squeak **rang** out through a **bullhorn**. "We're ready! Let's try the leaping scene!"

Colette, Paulina, Nicky, Pam, and Violet scurried toward the edge of the set to get a **better look**.

"Hey, what's that?" Violet asked, pointing to **oil spots** on the grass below the tower.

Pamela was right next to her. She looked around **CAREFULLY**, trying to figure out where the oil had come from.

"It's from the axle that holds the **cables** the stuntmouse will be hooked up to!" Pam cried. "It must be **worn out**. There's a good chance it will **break**, and the stuntmouse will fall!"

Violet and Pamela **caught up** with the other Thea Sisters and told them what they'd found.

What's that?

"We have to warn the stuntmouse right away!" Colette cried.

"He's already going up the tower," Pam said. "We'll never make it in TIME!"

The mouselets looked *around*. There was no time to ask for help — they had to figure out a solution on their own.

"I've got it!" Colette exclaimed. "See those bags full of **leaves** over there?" She pointed to some bags not far from where the stuntmouse was supposed to land. "We could . . ."

"Move them to cushion his FALL!" Pam finished her friend's sentence.

"Exactly!" Colette said.

Pam and Nicky sprang into action. They raced over to the BAGS of leaves and began dragging them toward the base of the tower.

Come on, let's move one more!

Phew ... these are heavy!

The other Thea Sisters hurried over to Charlie Cinerat, trying to warn him of the DANGER. But the stuntmouse leaped before they reached the director.

Colette closed her eyes; she couldn't bear to look. The other Thea Sisters held their breath . . .

"Smoking Swiss cheese, the AXLE is cracking!" the director shouted.

At that moment, the stuntmouse fell. The whole crew looked on in **HORROR**. But it was too late for anyone to do anything.

There was an awful moment of silence as the stuntmouse tumbled through the air. And then . . . he landed right on the bags of leaves!

"Thank goodmouse!" Paulina rejoiced.

Colette opened one eye, and then the other. "NICE SAVE, MOUSELETS!"

Ouchie ouch . . . What just happened?!

A DISASTROUS DAY!

Charlie Cinerat ran over to check on the stuntmouse. Once the director had made sure he was okay, he turned to the Thea Sisters. "Mouselets, I don't know what just happened, but it's all because of you that nobody got hurt! How can I t**HaNK** you?"

"Oh, you don't have to do anything. We're just glad the stuntmouse is —" Paulina began.

"Actually," Colette cut in. "There is something you can do. We'd really love a((-acce§§ passes to the set. We want to learn how movies are made."

"You got it!" the director replied.

"Go Coco!" Pam murmured. "This is going to be **absolutely fabumouse**!"

Meanwhile, on the other side of campus, Dylan was **grumpier** than a groundhog. The ratlet had followed the Ruby Crew across campus, hoping for a chance to talk to Connie.

But Ruby wouldn't leave him *alone*! She was squeaking Dylan's ear off, hoping to impress him.

I have a natural gift for acting, so . . .

"I've always liked acting," Ruby began, "and everyone noticed my **NATURAL** talent when . . . **blah blah blah** . . . and then I scored a part in . . ." Ruby went on and on. She was hoping Dylan would use his connections to get her access to the **MOVIE** world.

"I have an **idea**!" Ruby babbled. "We could **rehearse** some scenes from my favorite films together!" As she recited a list of

Ruby in
TITANIC

Ruby in
ROMAN HOLIDAY

titles, she pictured herself appearing in those **movies** with Dylan.

"Ruby," Dylan interrupted at last. "I'm really **BUSY**. I don't think I'll have time."

Before he could finish, Ruby burst into **TEARS**.

"I didn't mean to upset you," said Dylan, his tail sagging with embarrassment. He looked at Connie for help. But when he tried to comfort Ruby, a wide smile spread across her snout.

"Pretty good, right?" she said.

Now Dylan's tail was really in a twist. Ruby had been acting — she faked her tears!

Just then the Thea Sisters arrived. Dylan seized the chance to talk to Connie while Ruby was DISTRACTED.

But the harder Dylan tried, the WORSE it got. Every word he squeaked made him sound conceited and SNOTTY!

Colette glanced over at Dylan and Connie. Despite his SNOOTY SNOUT, she was sure there was something else going on.

LiGHTS...
CAMERA...
ACTiON!

That night, there was an icy **WIND** on Whale Island. Half the students were up late, looking out their windows. They were all hoping it wouldn't rain. The movie set had not been built sturdily enough to withstand much **DAMAGE**. If it rained, the next day's filming would have to be postponed.

But in the morning, the CLOUDS were gone. A chilly wind was blowing, but the SUN was bright in the sky. That meant the show could go on!

Faster than the mouse that ran up the clock, the students hurried to the garden.

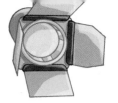

"Are you nervous?" Violet asked Kiki.

"Yes, of course I am," the mouselet replied. "My paws aren't shaking like they used to, but I'm always a little nervous before we begin filming."

A moment later, the assistant director scurried over and pawed Kiki some papers. "Here's the SCRIPT of the scene we're about to shoot. Take a quick peek."

Kiki had already memorized all her **LINES** for the scene, but she gave the script a **LOOK** anyway.

"It's the scene when Victor's friend Emmy finds out he wants to leave," Pam said.

"And Summer decides to go with him because she's in love with him," Colette continued.

VICTOR

I've already made up my mind: I have to leave!

EMMY

Where are you going to go?

VICTOR

I don't know yet, but I can't stay in this town. Soon everyone will know my secret.

SUMMER

If you go away, I will go with you.

EMMY

Summer, you can't!

SUMMER

I could never stay here without Victor. I have to go with him — I have no choice.

*A*h-ah-ah-**CHOO!**

Just then a loud sneeze echoed across the garden. A moment later, Mary, the actor playing Emmy, scurried onto the set.

"Hi, Kiki," she said with a stuffy-sounding squeak.

"Mary, are you okay?" asked Kiki, **worried**.

Mary blew her snout loudly. "Yes, yes, I'm all right. I caught a little **COLD**, but I just had a nice cup of hot cheese, and I'll be fine in no time."

The mouselets' friend Craig was helping Charlie Cinerat **ORGANIZE** the actors. He scampered over to Kiki and Mary. "We're about to start the shoot," he announced.

The two **mouselets** headed toward the set. The Thea Sisters joined the Ruby Crew at the back of the **garden**.

Professor Ratyshnikov and Professor Plotfur were in the audience, too. Everyone was EAGER to see the two famous actors at work.

The assistant director cried, "**TAKE ONE!**"

"Action!" Charlie Cinerat called.

Dylan recited his first line: "I've already made up my mind. I have to leave!"

Colette, Nicky, Pam, Paulina, and Violet were IMPRESSED: In the space of just a few seconds, Dylan was completely in **character**.

Unfortunately, when it was Mary's turn . . .

"Where are you GOING to . . . ACHOO!"

The mouselet couldn't even finish her line before a sneeze overcame her. And it got worse: A minute later, her **fur** was covered with red bumps.

"That's no cold . . . Mary is having an allergy attack!" Kiki exclaimed.

"I'll call a doctor," the assistant director said.

"We can't go on like this!" Charlie Cinerat shouted. He buried his snout in his paws. "What a cat-astrophe!"

A few **crew members** gathered around Charlie Cinerat to calm him down.

Dylan took off his **jacket** and put it around Mary's shoulders. "You'll feel **better** in a minute," he told her. "Let's go

What a cat-astrophe!

back to your room and wait for the **doctor**. You need to rest and get off your paws."

The Thea Sisters and the Ruby Crew were touched by the ratlet's *kindness* and consideration. *He usually seems so uppity,* Connie thought. *Maybe I was wrong about him after all.*

Kiki tried to convince Charlie Cinerat to postpone the shoot for a few days, until Mary was back on her paws.

"We can't postpone," the director moaned. "We're already over budget! We have to find a way to continue."

That gave Kiki an IDEA. "The part Mary was supposed to play isn't that hard. Maybe you could find a mouselet from the academy who could take the role," she suggested.

Charlie Cinerat looked **doubtful**. He

shook his snout. "I don't think so, Kiki . . ."

"It could take Mary a while to **get better**," the assistant director pointed out.

At that, the director gave in. "Putrid cheese puffs, I can't take it anymore! Okay, you're right. Let's hold an audition tomorrow."

Let's hold an audition.

LOOKS CAN BE DECEIVING

A few hours later, when the shoot was finished for the day, the Thea Sisters caught up with Kiki to CONGRATULATE her. Despite that morning's setback, she and Dylan had continued filming the SCENES that Mary's character wasn't a part of. The two actors were both very *talented* on their own, but together, there was a special sparkle to their scenes. They had an AMAZING connection and chemistry.

"You and Dylan were super!" Nicky exclaimed.

"When I watch you

act, I almost forget where I am. I felt like I was standing in the moonlight with Victor and Summer," Colette added.

"Oh, I'm just LUCKY," Kiki said, blushing to the roots of her fur. "Working with Dylan makes everything easier. He's super talented, plus he's a FANTASTIC ratlet to boot!"

Colette had never really believed that Dylan was a SNOOTYSNOUT. But she was still curious to get Kiki's take on him. "Today Dylan was so sweet to Mary. But yesterday he seemed colder than the Abominable Snowmouse . . ."

Kiki laughed. "Let me tell you a story about Dylan. When I first met him three years ago, I had the same impression. He seemed snotty and downright stuck-up! I was sure that working with him was going to be **AWFUL**."

"So what changed your mind?" Paulina asked.

"Nothing!" Kiki said. "Except I got to know him better. And I realized some rodents need a bit more TIME to show you who they really are. Dylan is very shy, and that makes him seem UNFRIENDLY at first. But, in fact, he is one of the most generous ratlets I've ever met."

"You're right, Kiki. You can't judge a rodent by his fur," said Pam, FROWNING. "We shouldn't have jumped to conclusions about Dylan."

While Kiki and the Thea Sisters were talking, the sun had set.

"What do you think about heading back to my room for a snack? I have a fresh box of Cheesy Chews," Colette told Kiki.

"Sure, that sounds great," Kiki replied

enthusiastically.

"Yay!" Colette said. "And maybe we can squeeze in a quick pawicure, too! I really want to show you my kit. It has over **153** different shades of **PINK** polish!"

"Colette, that sounds *paw*-sitively perfect!" Kiki said, grinning at her new friend.

Which do you prefer — Cotton Candy or Pretty in Pink?

ACTOR WANTED!

Most **mornings**, there was **mayhem** in the Mouseford dorms. The students would stumble out of their rooms, stretching their tails, and chat with one another, making plans for the day.

But the next morning, the dorms were so **QUIET** you could hear a cheddar cheese slice drop.

"Is everyone still **ASLEEP**?" Paulina asked as she and the other Thea Sisters **SCAMPERED** down to the Great Hall.

"The auditions will begin in an hour. Maybe everyone's getting ready," Violet said, shrugging.

It was only when they *reached* the Great Hall that the mouselets understood what was going on. News of the audition had spread across campus *FASTER* than the smell of melting cheese. Nearly every single student at Mouseford had **risen** earlier than usual and scurried over. Most were there to participate, but others had just come to watch the audition.

"So this is where everyone is!" Pam said.

"Hey, isn't that Ruby's assistant?!" said Nicky, pointing to a tall, *dignified-looking* ratlet. "What's he doing here?"

"Well, I don't think he's here to try out," Pam put in.

"Alan is waiting in **line** for me," Ruby explained, coming up behind them. "You know the old saying: The early mouse gets the cheese! But naturally, I had no desire to wait for **HOURS** to audition. I need my beauty sleep! I told Alan to spend

I'm so sleepy!

the **NIGHT** here so I could go first."

Colette rolled her eyes. It was just like Ruby to get someone to do her dirty work for her!

The door at the end of the **HALLWAY** opened, and Professor Plotfur and Charlie Cinerat appeared.

"Everyone ready?" Professor Plotfur asked. "We're about to begin!"

A TERRIBLE TRYOUT

Colette, Nicky, Pam, Paulina, and Violet found seats in the **audience** behind Charlie Cinerat and Professor Plotfur, who were set to judge the aspiring **actors**. The mouselets weren't going to **AUDiTiON**, but they were interested in observing the selection process.

The first one to step onstage was Ruby. Dylan followed in her pawsteps. He'd offered to **help** the candidates run their lines.

"Okay," Professor Plotfur announced, "we can start."

Ruby started right after Dylan read his first line.

But her squeak was **shaky**, and she put extra stress on every word, which made her character sound more nervous than a rodent in a lion's den.

"Ruby's too anxious. She's not doing her best," Colette whispered.

At that moment, Ruby *threw her paws* around Dylan. She was trying to bring extra feeling to her last line, but it felt all wrong for the character.

"I'd say she's doing her worst!" Pamela put in. She was a little DISMAYED by Ruby's performance. It was clear Ruby was tenser than a rat in a cat clinic.

When the audition ended, Ruby SCURRIED offstage and out the door of the Great Hall. She tried to hide her disappointment with a **confident** smile, but she wasn't pleased with her performance.

I could have done better...

Ruby knew what she had to do. She had to ask for another chance to read the scene. The **EXCITEMENT** of going first had messed with her snout.

But when she opened the door to go back in, she realized Dylan was talking about her. Quiet as a mouse, she stopped to listen.

"I don't think Ruby is the actor we're looking for. I spent time with her, and she's a real **show-off**," Dylan was telling Charlie Cinerat.

When she heard that, Ruby was crushed. "Me, a show-off?" she huffed. Then she scurried away. She didn't want anyone to know she'd been listening in.

"Ruby's audition wasn't good, but I think she was just nervous," Professor Plotfur told Dylan.

"I know we don't always see snout-to-snout with Ruby, but I hate to see her get eliminated like that," Paulina whispered to Pamela.

"You said it, sis," Pam agreed. "Professor Plotfur is right: Ruby is a good actor. But it's not up to us . . ."

WHAT A DISAPPOINTMENT!

Outside the Great Hall, Ruby started looking for Alicia, Connie, and Zoe. She wanted to tell her friends about the GREAT INJUSTICE that had been done to her. "If I don't get the part, it's all Dylan's fault! He told Charlie Cinerat NOT to pick me!"

The Ruby Crew was outraged, especially Connie. She'd started to see Dylan differently after he'd been so kind to Mary. Now she didn't know what to THINK.

"But how did your audition go?" Connie asked, confused.

"What do you mean?" Zoe asked. "Of course Ruby was awesome! She's the BEST actor in our year!"

While Ruby was complaining about Dylan, the **AUDITIONS** continued inside the Great Hall. When it was Connie's turn, the mouselet strode into the Great Hall with a **FURIOUS** look on her snout.

"What's up with Connie?" Pamela asked.

"She looks madder than a mouse with a trap on his or her tail," Nicky agreed.

Connie stalked *ONSTAGE*, but she had no intention of reading lines from the scene. As soon as Dylan delivered his first line, she snapped, "You are nothing but a spoiled, STUCK-UP snootysnout!"

The Thea Sisters exchanged looks: Connie was way **overreacting**! Dylan didn't deserve to be treated like that.

"I don't understand. Why is Connie so upset?" Kiki asked Colette.

Colette took a careful look at Connie.

Despite the **angry** expression on her snout, her eyes were sad.

"I don't think she's angry. I think she's *disappointed*," Colette said. "You know what? I think she actually **CARES** about Dylan, and she's upset about the way he squeaked about Ruby."

After **CHEWING** Dylan out, Connie scampered off, leaving the movie star totally **dumbstruck**. In fact, he had been totally **SQUEAKLESS** from the moment Connie walked in.

"I can't do this anymore," he told Charlie Cinerat. Then he **HEADED** for the door.

The director jumped up. "What do you mean? Come back here right away! We need **YOU**!" he shouted. But Dylan wasn't listening.

Come back!

"Mouselets, are you *thinking* what I'm thinking?" Violet asked, leaning in close to her friends.

This is a cat-astrophe!

Colette smiled and nodded. "We've got to help!" she said. "Friends together, mice forever!"

A NEW FRIEND

The auditions continued without Dylan. There were a **LOT** of mouselets who wanted their shot at the silver screen. And the chance to act next to Dylan and Kiki was hard to pass up!

As soon as Charlie Cinerat suggested a break, the Thea Sisters scurried out of the Great Hall.

"I think Connie made the same **MISTAKE** we did. She thought Dylan's shyness was snobbishness," Nicky said.

Paulina had an **IDEA**. "Let's see if we can find him. Maybe we can convince him to go talk to Connie."

Colette, Nicky, Pam, and Violet agreed. They decided to **LOOK** for Dylan together.

It didn't take them long to **find** the ratlet. He was in the garden, reviewing his **script** of the next day's scenes.

Dylan was so **focused** on his lines that it took him a moment to realize the Thea Sisters were standing in front of him.

"Hey!" Pam exclaimed, trying to get his **attention**.

"Oh . . . hi," Dylan replied, trying to smile.

Colette noticed the **sadness** on his snout, and she got straight to the point. "Dylan, we saw what happened with Connie. You have to go talk to her."

Connie is mad at me!

Dylan **HESITATED**: "I . . . well . . . really . . . you see . . ."

That's when Violet squeaked up. "Dylan, I know what you're feeling, because it's happened to me, too," she said, sitting down next to him. "Other rodents often *misunderstand* my **shyness**. But if you want to make things right, all you need is a little COURAGE. Show Connie your true self, and she'll see you didn't mean to hurt Ruby or anyone."

"I don't think that Connie wants to talk to me anymore," Dylan said, his whiskers **DROOPING**.

"Actually, I think she does," Paulina chimed in.

Violet nodded. "She wouldn't get up in your snout if she didn't think you were a good rodent at heart."

"She'll be **happy** to find out she was wrong about you," Colette agreed.

Dylan wasn't so **SURE** Connie would give him

You can do it!

Thanks!

another CHANCE. But the Thea Sisters convinced him to try.

"Try **OPENING UP** to her. I'm sure she'll listen," Violet urged him.

"Thanks," Dylan replied gratefully.

Pamela shook his paw. "That's what friends are for!" She helped him up, and then added, "The next round of auditions is about to begin. They need you in the Great Hall right away!"

ANOTHER CHANCE

The tryouts went on for the rest of the morning. With Dylan's **help**, the remaining mouselets were able to do their best. With a few kind **words** or a simple smile, he made the **hopeful** actors feel comfortable.

After watching the last audition, the Thea Sisters decided to go talk to the **director**. They wanted him to give Ruby another chance. They'd had their differences with Ruby before, but they knew how excited she was about the movie. And they also knew she was a talented actor.

Will you come with me?

Yes!

"Ruby can be a show-off, it's true. But she is a really GOOD actor," Colette told Charlie Cinerat.

"She was nervous because she went first, but if you give her another chance, you'll see. When it comes to acting, she's the real deal," Nicky added.

The Thea Sisters were so **convincing** that the director **relented**. "Okay, tell her to come back," he said.

The Thea Sisters wasted no time. They scampered off to tell Ruby. A few minutes later, she was back in the Great Hall.

We did it!

Ruby was thrilled to get a second shot at auditioning.

"**THANK YOU**," Ruby whispered to the Thea Sisters. "I owe you one!"

"We'll remember you said that," said Nicky, winking.

Before Ruby started her audition, Dylan gave her some advice.

"Don't be nervous," he told her. "Forget you're onstage; forget all about the audience.

Forget you're onstage— forget about everything!

In fact, forget about everything. Now take a deep breath and **GET OUT THERE!**"

Dylan was so busy talking to Ruby that he didn't realize Connie had joined them. The **mouselet** listened to the advice Dylan was giving her friend, and she realized she'd made an **ENORMOUSE** mistake in judging him. But how could she make it up to him now? After her earlier OUTBURST, he would never forgive her!

"Are you ready?" Charlie Cinerat asked Ruby.

Ruby scurried onstage and looked around her, **FRIGHTENED**. This was her last chance — she couldn't afford to make another mistake.

Then Ruby remembered what Dylan had told her. She let his words sink in. And when it was her turn to squeak, the world around her seemed to DISAPPEAR. She completely inhabited the role of Emmy.

Ruby's audition was incredible, and Charlie Cinerat had no doubts: The part was hers!

LiKE HoNEY AND LEMoN

After the audition was over, the Thea Sisters met up in Colette and Pam's room. They still wanted to find a way to fix the friendship between Dylan and Connie.

"If we could just find a WAY to get Dylan to go talk to Connie, she'd see he's really a nice ratlet!" said Colette. "And then everything will be okay again."

Pam fell onto her bed with a sigh. "If we can just get them in the SAME place at the SAME time, it'll fix itself."

"You're right, Pam," said Colette. "Just like honey and lemon!"

Nicky, Pam, Paulina, and Violet all shot Colette PUZZLED looks. Finally, Paulina squeaked for them all. "What do HONEY and lemon have to do with it?"

Colette scrambled out of her chair. "Honey and lemon are two ingredients that don't seem to go well together, but if you put them in a bowl and mix them, you get an amazing SNOUT MASK."

"And a perfect way to spice up a good snack," Pam put in, grinning.

"Colette!" Paulina exclaimed. "Don't tell me you're thinking of starting a new beauty treatment right now, are you?"

"Of course I'm not!" Colette replied. "Connie is the honey, Dylan is the lemon, and the bowl is a nice, romantic spot where they can meet!"

"A romantic spot . . ." Nicky mused.

"The North Tower," Violet cut in. "There's a beautiful VIEW from up there!"

It was decided. They had to find a way to

get Dylan and Connie to meet at the North Tower.

The mouselets put their snouts together until they **came up** with a plan. Colette, Violet, and Nicky would find a way to get Connie there, and Pam and Paulina would enlist Kiki to get Dylan to join her.

"**Come on**!" Colette exclaimed. "Move those paws, mouselings! Let's get to work!"

A NEW BEGINNING

"Why in the name of string cheese would I want to CLIMB the North Tower?" Connie asked.

Colette, Nicky, and Violet glanced at one another, tails twitching with embarrassment.

"Because . . . there is someone waiting for you at the top," Nicky said at last.

Connie was SUSPICIOUS. "And who is this someone?"

"We can't tell you," Colette said.

"You just have to trust us!" Violet put in.

The three mouselets were so persistent that Connie eventually gave in. She SCAMPERED across campus to keep her mysterious appointment.

I shouldn't trust those three rodents, she

thought as she scrambled up the **TOWER**. *They're probably just pulling my paw . . .*

At last, she reached the last flight of stairs. There was a note waiting for her.

"Just a few more steps," she read out loud.

Now her curiosity was getting the best of her. In the blink of a cat's eye, she **climbed** the steps and reached the tower room, where Dylan was waiting.

The **RATLET** did not give her a chance to squeak. He stuck out his paw. "Hi, I'm Dylan. I know I might look **snooty**, but I'm actually just very *SHY*."

You see, Dylan was hoping to begin again with Connie. And this time, he wanted to **show her** who he really was.

A note?!

Connie melted like mozzarella on a hot summer's day. "Hi, I'm Connie, and when I get angry I can make a terrible SCENE!" she replied, smiling.

The two rodents burst out laughing. Soon they were both as relaxed as a couple of rats in a cheese shop, and they started talking and joking around like old friends.

The Thea Sisters and Kiki were down in the garden. They couldn't see what was going on up in the tower, but when they heard the sound of laughter, they knew their plan had worked.

"True friends are worth their weight in Brie," Colette said happily.

"You are so right, Coco!" Kiki exclaimed. "I feel really lucky to have made good buddies like you. You and the Ruby Crew must be my guests for the world premiere of

Two Mice in the Moonlight!"

The Thea Sisters were squeakless. They threw their paws around Kiki for a big **group hug**.

"I guess that's a yes!" said Kiki, laughing.

Hooray!

A DREAM, OR REALITY?

At last, it was the day of the world premiere of *Two Mice in the Moonlight*, and the THEA SISTERS were racing through the airport.

"Scurry up, mouselings, we're running late!" Pamela exclaimed, leading the way to the **DEPARTURE LOUNGE**. "Our plane is about to take off!"

The Thea Sisters and the Ruby Crew were all booked on the same **FLIGHT** to Los Angeles.

The mouselets barely made it to the plane on time. Once there, they breathed a sigh of relief.

"I could use a nice ratnap to recover from this *RUN*!" Paulina puffed.

"Check it out. Violet's already got a head

start," Pam joked, **POINTING** to her friend, who'd closed her eyes the moment she got on the plane.

When they arrived in Los Angeles, the mouselets rushed to the hotel to put on the evening dresses they'd so carefully selected.

Once they were all dressed and ready, they scrambled downstairs and found a **big car** waiting for them.

How thrilling!

"**WOW!**" Alicia exclaimed, admiring the shiny limousine. "This is cooler than iced cheese on a hot summer's day!"

"Good evening, mouselets," the *driver* said with a smile, opening the door. "Please take your seats."

The Thea Sisters thought they were living in a *dream*. But when they finally spotted Kiki and Dylan again, they realized it was real.

They had made two true new friends!

Don't miss
any of these
exciting
Thea Sisters
adventures!

Thea Stilton and the
Dragon's Code

Thea Stilton and the
Mountain of Fire

Thea Stilton and the
Ghost of the Shipwreck

Thea Stilton and the
Secret City

Thea Stilton and the
Mystery in Paris

Thea Stilton and the
Cherry Blossom Adventure

Thea Stilton and the
Star Castaways

Thea Stilton: Big Trouble
in the Big Apple

Thea Stilton and the
Ice Treasure

Thea Stilton and the
Secret of the Old Castle

Thea Stilton and the
Blue Scarab Hunt

Thea Stilton and the
Prince's Emerald

Thea Stilton and the
Mystery on the Orient Express

Thea Stilton and the
Dancing Shadows

Thea Stilton and the
Legend of the Fire Flowers

Thea Stilton and the
Spanish Dance Mission

Thea Stilton and the
Journey to the Lion's Den

Thea Stilton and the
Great Tulip Heist

Thea Stilton and the
Chocolate Sabotage

Thea Stilton and the
Missing Myth

Thea Stilton and the
Lost Letters

Thea Stilton and the
Tropical Treasure

Thea Stilton and the
Hollywood Hoax

Thea Stilton and the
Madagascar Madness

Don't miss any of these Mouseford Academy adventures!

#1 Drama at Mouseford

#2 The Missing Diary

#3 Mouselets in Danger

#4 Dance Challenge

#5 The Secret Invention

#6 A Mouseford Musical

#7 Mice Take the Stage

#8 A Fashionable Mystery

#9 The Mysterious Love Letter

#10 A Dream on Ice

#11 Lights, Camera, Action!

#12 Mice on the Runway

Be sure to read all my fabumouse adventures!

#1 Lost Treasure of the Emerald Eye

#2 The Curse of the Cheese Pyramid

#3 Cat and Mouse in a Haunted House

#4 I'm Too Fond of My Fur!

#5 Four Mice Deep in the Jungle

#6 Paws Off, Cheddarface!

#7 Red Pizzas for a Blue Count

#8 Attack of the Bandit Cats

#9 A Fabumouse Vacation for Geronimo

#10 All Because of a Cup of Coffee

#11 It's Halloween, You 'Fraidy Mouse!

#12 Merry Christmas, Geronimo!

#13 The Phantom of the Subway

#14 The Temple of the Ruby of Fire

#15 The Mona Mousa Code

#16 A Cheese-Colored Camper

#17 Watch Your Whiskers, Stilton!

#18 Shipwreck on the Pirate Islands

#19 My Name Is Stilton, Geronimo Stilton

#20 Surf's Up, Geronimo!

#21 The Wild, Wild West

#22 The Secret of Cacklefur Castle

A Christmas Tale

 **#23 Valentine's Day Disaster**

 **#24 Field Trip to Niagara Falls**

#25 The Search for Sunken Treasure

 **#26 The Mummy with No Name**

 **#27 The Christmas Toy Factory**

 **#28 Wedding Crasher**

 **#29 Down and Out Down Under**

 **#30 The Mouse Island Marathon**

 **#31 The Mysterious Cheese Thief**

 **Christmas Catastrophe**

 **#32 Valley of the Giant Skeletons**

 **#33 Geronimo and the Gold Medal Mystery**

 **#34 Geronimo Stilton, Secret Agent**

 **#35 A Very Merry Christmas**

 **#36 Geronimo's Valentine**

 **#37 The Race Across America**

 **#38 A Fabumouse School Adventure**

 **#39 Singing Sensation**

 **#40 The Karate Mouse**

 **#41 Mighty Mount Kilimanjaro**

 **#42 The Peculiar Pumpkin Thief**

 **#43 I'm Not a Supermouse!**

 **#44 The Giant Diamond Robbery**

 **#45 Save the White Whale!**

 **#46 The Haunted Castle**

#47 Run for the Hills, Geronimo! **#48 The Mystery in Venice** **#49 The Way of the Samurai** **#50 This Hotel Is Haunted!** **#51 The Enormouse Pearl Heist**

#52 Mouse in Space! **#53 Rumble in the Jungle** **#54 Get into Gear, Stilton!** **#55 The Golden Statue Plot** **#56 Flight of the Red Bandit**

The Hunt for the Golden Book **#57 The Stinky Cheese Vacation** **#58 The Super Chef Contest** **#59 Welcome to Moldy Manor** **The Hunt for the Curious Cheese**

#60 The Treasure of Easter Island **#61 Mouse House Hunter** **#62 Mouse Overboard!** **The Hunt for the Secret Papyrus** **#63 The Cheese Experiment**

#64 Magical Mission **#65 Bollywood Burglary** **The Hunt for the Hundredth Key**

Be sure to read all of our magical special edition adventures!

THE KINGDOM OF FANTASY

THE QUEST FOR PARADISE:
THE RETURN TO THE KINGDOM OF FANTASY

THE AMAZING VOYAGE:
THE THIRD ADVENTURE IN THE KINGDOM OF FANTASY

THE DRAGON PROPHECY:
THE FOURTH ADVENTURE IN THE KINGDOM OF FANTASY

THE VOLCANO OF FIRE:
THE FIFTH ADVENTURE IN THE KINGDOM OF FANTASY

THE SEARCH FOR TREASURE:
THE SIXTH ADVENTURE IN THE KINGDOM OF FANTASY

THE ENCHANTED CHARMS:
THE SEVENTH ADVENTURE IN THE KINGDOM OF FANTASY

THE PHOENIX OF DESTINY:
AN EPIC KINGDOM OF FANTASY ADVENTURE

THE HOUR OF MAGIC:
THE EIGHTH ADVENTURE IN THE KINGDOM OF FANTASY

THE WIZARD'S WAND:
THE NINTH ADVENTURE IN THE KINGDOM OF FANTASY

THEA STILTON: THE JOURNEY TO ATLANTIS

THEA STILTON: THE SECRET OF THE FAIRIES

THEA STILTON: THE SECRET OF THE SNOW

THEA STILTON: THE CLOUD CASTLE

THEA STILTON: THE TREASURE OF THE SEA

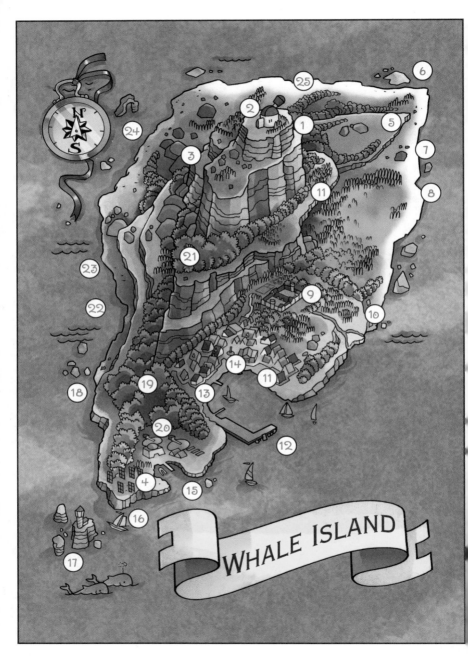

WHALE ISLAND

MAP OF WHALE ISLAND

1. Falcon Peak
2. Observatory
3. Mount Landslide
4. Solar Energy Plant
5. Ram Plain
6. Very Windy Point
7. Turtle Beach
8. Beachy Beach
9. Mouseford Academy
10. Kneecap River
11. Mariner's Inn
12. Port
13. Squid House
14. Town Square
15. Butterfly Bay
16. Mussel Point
17. Lighthouse Cliff
18. Pelican Cliff
19. Nightingale Woods
20. Marine Biology Lab
21. Hawk Woods
22. Windy Grotto
23. Seal Grotto
24. Seagulls Bay
25. Seashell Beach

THANKS FOR READING,
AND GOOD-BYE UNTIL OUR
NEXT ADVENTURE!

TheaSisters